AS I EVOLVE

A Collection of Poetry

Darcel Stacy Ann Joseph

Foreword

As I Evolve is a compilation of poetry written by Darcel Joseph.

The title is indeed fitting as this is a work that developed over time, even as the author herself was changing and growing mentally, emotionally and spiritually.

As one reads the poems it is impossible to miss the poet's conflict within, as she considers and attempts to comprehend personal challenges as well as the hardships others experience. What is also evident is her faith in God and her dependence on Him in all circumstances.

Darcel's poems will touch the heart of the reader, bringing warmth and a sense of calm to their soul as they read. She addresses real issues in her pieces, issues of broken relationships, abuse, discrimination, to mention a few. However, the thing that makes her work appealing, certainly uplifting, is the themes that are infused in the poems, that being, God's love for mankind and His transforming power.

Her pieces will give hope and a different perspective to the reader as she gently or subtly invites him to look to God even in the most difficult of situations.

As I Evolve is a book that can be appreciated by anyone. In a world where people are constantly bombarded with such negativity, it is truly refreshing to release to this space something that brings optimism and that injects a bit of faith in our lives. I think we can all benefit from this work of love.

Rhonda Redhead- Brathwaite
Literature Teacher

About the Author

Darcel Joseph is a child of the Most High God. She is the Founder and Executive Director of a Non-Governmental Organization, Children of the Promise Foundation (CPF). Darcel has a great passion for children and youths and desires that life-changing impact will be made and seen in the life of each individual who interacts with CPF.

Additionally, she hopes to nurture and develop transformational leaders, through programs facilitated by CPF. Darcel holds a Bachelor of Arts Degree in Psychology and Counselling and a Master's Degree in Christian Ministry. She also has supplemental certification in Social Work, Confident Parenting, and Youth Harvest Training.

Darcel has over fourteen years of experience in the Social Services field, where she worked in the areas of food security, child protection as well individual and family trauma. Through this, she learned how to intervene and advocate for indigent and at-risk members of society. Although fairly new to the NGO and Social Enterprise field, Darcel and her team have made tremendous strides.

Through partnerships with local and international organizations such as, Initiatives of Change USA, Unit Trust Corporation (UTC), Eastern Credit Union, Republic Bank Limited, Branford General Contractors, and Telecommunication Services of Trinidad and Tobago (TSTT). Darcel has spearheaded a movement that assists numerous disadvantaged families throughout Trinidad and Tobago.

Darcel is an alumna of the International Exchange Research Board (IREX) Community Solutions Program and Initiatives of Change -

AP, Caux Scholars Program. Both experiences she describes as transitional, life-changing, and mind-blowing.

Though quiet and humble by nature, Darcel is also adventurous, enjoys traveling, experiencing new cultures, and spending time with loved ones and friends. She believes that people are placed on the earth for a purpose that is far greater than themselves and that truly Each One Can Reach One.

Book Design and Illustrations

by

Jooneyd

To connect with the designer to hire

Fiverr Profile Link

https://www.fiverr.com/jooneydraza

LinkedIn Profile Link

https://www.linkedin.com/in/jooneydraza/

Table of Contents

When I Write 9

What Do You Write? 10

Trials 11

Twisted 12

The Way I See It 13

Victim 14

Advocate 15

Thinking Out Loud 17

Desires 18

Woman 19

Be My Guide 21

Hope in God 23

He Died For Me 24

The Dialogue 25

Do You See Me? 28

Father 30

That's My Mother 31

To My Promise 32

Em City 33

By His Stripes 34

Dougla 36

Behind these Prison Walls 38

The Wait 40

If I can Change my Hair 41

He Loves Me 42

My Daddy, my Papa, my Oh… 43

Sound the Alarm 45

God's Got Me 47

Musings of a Worshipper 49

The Fight 50

When I Write

When I write I open up
I reach a whole new level
I get a better understanding of my feelings.
When I write, my soul opens up
I free myself one word at a time.

When I write, I get to know the real me
The me that isn't afraid to speak.
The me that doesn't have to be
The perfect friend, girlfriend, or daughter.
The me that can let her thoughts out
Without hindrance or fear.

Writing, to me is a dream.
Can anyone relate to what I mean?

What Do You Write?

What do you write when you don't know what to write?
When your mind is in a bind and you don't know where to start.
What do say when you don't what to say?
When the thoughts are so much that when you talk the convo strays.

How do you explain, things that you don't quite understand?
When you have more questions than answers
And things seem too big for you to fathom.

You trust then in your Father. The Creator of the world.
The One who sees and knows all things, and holds the future in His hands.
You ask Him to lead you, to teach you His will.
Trust that as His plans unfold, He'll hold your hand and guide your path.

Trials

Trials of life will come and go,
But if you continue to stand firm in God
He'll direct your path and show you where to go.

One day at a time is how it should be
Just keep your eyes fixed upon Christ.
Give unto Him, the little that you've got
He'll turn it around into more than you could ever want.

Know that He's loving you,
His hands forever upon you.
A companion and a friend
He's with you till the end.
In every situation
Remember that His grace is sufficient.

Twisted

There are things I think
and do not say.
There are things I notice
And yet do not see.
My feelings I know
Yet do not comprehend
Places I go
But still do not reach.

My mind in a rumble
Heart all twisted into knots.
Lord knows if it's busted.

I love to love
To be loved is nice.
But then again, how is love to be defined?

For my heart, I can't trust
No matter how I try.
My heart I can't say
To be the apple of anybody's eye.

Everything was twisted
All into a knot.
And the one to untwist it
Hopefully will be someone I can trust.

The Way I See It

Mothers in Court, awaiting milk money,
Daddy's with his girlfriend having a nice time.
Babies keep crying,
Cause' they're hungry
Five-year old's asking "mommy where daddy?"
That's the way I see it.

Murder and drug rates are sky high.
An eighteen-year-old is running wild
Grandmothers bawling "why oh why, they going to let this country die?"
That's the way I see it.

Boyfriends in jail
Girlfriends begging for bail.
Wondering if to let her mother know
That she is willing to kick the pail.
As her unborn baby silently wails
May I please live to see one bright day?
That's the way I see it.

Victim

He was all over me like a plague
He just refused to go away.
He made up his mind to hurt me
Destined to have his way.

His hands were all over me
Molding and caressing my body.
But his motive was not of love
Nor was it of passion.
His motive was only to destroy
That which no man had ever ploughed.

He laughed when he was finished
Quite pleased at what he'd done.
He was satisfied, he was proud
That he'd gotten a fresh one.

Away he went smiling
With not a care in the world.
Didn't even glance
At my limp body lying there.
Taking a part of my soul with him
To God alone knows where.

Advocate

I'm an advocate for those without a voice.
For those with so much pain and trauma
That sometimes the best way to take it out is on another.

I am an advocate.
For those whose hearts seemed filled with hate.
Self-hate, systemic hate, people hate.
They willingly trade love for hate
Simply because no one took the time to be compassionate.

Dreaded circumstances seem to dominate every hidden corner of their minds.
Searching for peace that seems so hard to find.
Searching for a way out
But they keep running into torrential doors.
Doors of oppression, aggression, frustration, and depression.
That ultimately leads to regression.
Doors of bitterness, shame, anger, hurt and pain
That keeps them in bondage, but their souls long to be salvaged.

I'm an advocate because someone advocated for me.
He dug deep down in the dust and said restoring my life is a must.
It must be worth living, after years of continually failing.
There must be a story that can give Him glory.
There must be some hope, and a better way to cope.

I am an advocate because Jesus Christ rescued me.
Now I am an advocate for those,
Who walk the road I once traveled upon.

Thinking Out Loud

Thinking of Home.
Sometimes I miss my friends, my family.
Me being here is a journey and I am learning to embrace it.
The journey is stepping out of my comfort zone.
Letting go of the familiar and opening up to the unknown.
I am curious about where to go from here?
What do I have to learn?
What do I embrace and what should I let go?
Embracing feels like learning to understand that
We are all human even if our faces differ.
I hope I can be who I was created to be.
To fulfill my life's purpose
While understanding that it's not all about me.

Desires

The beautiful moment of saying I do.
A walk in the park somewhere in Finland.
A bouncing baby boy who would call me mommy.
Twins, maybe triplets – who's counting babies are perfect.
Twilight movies, intimate dances
Whispered secrets with the one I love.
Early mornings, setting suns
Random things just for fun.
Shared visions, purposes fulfilled.
Moments of quietness.
Just to be still.

Woman

I am a woman
And out of my womb
Comes the future generation.
I am a woman
Beautifully shaped.
The happiness that I long for
Seems to be a constant struggle
That I'm sure you can see
Written on my face.

My father left home
When I was barely four.
My mother worked two jobs
And still, we were considered poor.
At sixteen my brother was murdered
Caught up in things that don't matter.
But I refuse to be among the numbers
I'll stand bold and say
I am proud to be a woman.

My body won't be sold
For riches and gold.
My dignity and pride
Reside forever at my side.
My face from you
I'll never have to hide.
For I am a woman
And I'll say it with style.

My husband promised to love me
Through sickness and health
Till death do us part
Were the words we spoke from our hearts.

He's proven to be faithful
Disrespect I won't condone
Cause I am a woman
Who knows what she brings to the table.

Two beautiful children that I bore
Bring me constant joy, I couldn't possibly ask for more.
My only regret
Is my first baby that I should have kept.
But now, I am emancipated
And I command nothing but respect.
For I am a woman
Who's brave enough to show it.

Be My Guide

To walk the road, I was called to walk
I must tarry along, only God can I trust.
I have heard His call
And while my heart was willing to say yes
My lifestyle said no.

Choose me God
I want to excel in you!
But it's not just about me being willing
God also rightly requires my obedience.

My silent prayer was to be holy
I need to live righteous!
This was the cry of my heart.
Yet, in bondage was I captured
Refusing to let go of that thing
I should not have desired.

Deliver me God
Turn me from my wicked ways.
Like one of your troubled flock
I have drifted away.
Draw me back
Like the shepherd you are.
And when I couldn't say a word
He listened to my heart.

My heart calls for out for healing
My soul thirsts for deliverance.
Yet it seems like
Here I am, once again
Standing amid the rain.

But alas!
Jesus did see me.
For in the hurt that threatens my hope.
And the disappointment, that could bring destruction.
I experience peace.
Now I can see the promise land
Look, its right there over the horizon.

Hope in God

Look at the tree, as it spreads its roots
So filled with hope and the promise of shade.
But the sun shines for days on end,
The leaves start to whither as the branches bend.
But alas God sends a shower of love
And that tree is blossoming once again.

Out of the balcony they look on
As the water gashes down the stream.
So pretty a picture
No one would have dreamed.
But soon the water rises
Higher ground their only refuge.
They scurry about trying to save
All their life's earnings from going down the drain.
Then, a rainbow appears
The promise is clear
God has answered their prayer.

Sounds of laughter fill the air
Young ones run about gaily, filled with not a care.
Music plays and rhythm sways
Dancers dance and lover's romance.
Then, a loud noise shatters through the air
They run for cover, but now it doesn't matter.
He has returned for the ones who were faithful.

He Died For Me

He died for me on Calvary
For my soul to be set free.
He purchased my salvation
His life was the cost.
To Him, I owe great honor
Much love and all respect.
For in my heart is His dwelling place
Where I can go to make amends.

The Dialogue

Inside there's a silent cry
Lord, please set me free.
Hear the faint voice of a dying child
Lord have mercy on me.

The storms rage and thunder billows
But He says my child, I am He.
Fears arise and joys are quelled
But He whispers,
Have hope in Me.

Look for Me, amid the pain
I'm at the center of all the heartache.
Keep your eyes on Me
Have I not promised
That never would I leave nor forsake thee?

My eyes once focused, struggle to see.
Lord, can You hear me?
Do You hear the words I cannot speak?
Can You feel my heart that sometimes retreats?
He says, My child, be still in Me.

Do You see the struggle to break free?
Of dreams untold and visions unspoken.
Observing one's life from an outer exterior
Not fully understanding how it all goes through the filter.

My child, please wait on Me.
I knew you before you were in your mother's womb
I created you to bring glory to Me.
Delight in Me, and do My will

I promise all that you desire will be fulfilled.

An upward climb, an ongoing journey.
Yet moments of happiness and peace
Seem to be sniffed out by the enemy.
But in the midst a quiet voice whisper
Will you trust Me?

Trust? What does one do when trusting fails?
When what you hoped for dies
And life turns out to be a raging fury?
So, He says, pick up your cross and tarry.
Follow after me wholeheartedly,
I'm prepared to lead you to a land
Flowing with milk and honey.

And when the rain subsides
Once more we find joy inside.
The sun brings warmth
So, we face the morrow
Knowing that weeping only endured the night.

But He says, I need you to trust Me
Where you cannot trace Me.
To know that even when it appears to be dark
and gloomy
I am still the risen Bridegroom.
And though you may not always understand
Know that I have a master plan.

I would lead you to the Promised Land
Come, my child, hold my hand.
Let Me be your constant guide
I would show you the truest definition of the term
'Ride or die'.
So together we say:

One step at a time
It's You and me.
You are my priority
My dialogue, and my song.
You are my heart,
You are my chosen one!

Do You See Me?

What do you see when you look at me?
Do you see my face do you see me?
Do you see the hurt and pain I feel?
Or do you just see someone strung out on drugs and a dirty demeanor?

When you look at me, what do you see?
Do you see the lashes that I took?
When I told him to stop but my innocence he ignored.
Or do you see the time my mother left without looking back.
Do you see my grandmother saying, my child don't fret?

What do you see when you look at me?
Do you see the tears that hide behind the smile?
Or do you see the representation of someone who couldn't care less.
The silly kid who makes bad choices
Leaving the seemingly smart adults to say "I wonder".

Maybe next time you see me, you should say hello.
Try asking how I've been and what led me to this place
Instead of coming to a conclusion by judging what you see on my face.

I am a human being
A child desiring to be set free.
How would you know if you can help?

If you don't ask me
Come, look in my eyes and tell me what you see.

Father

To me, you are a blessing
Provided by the Lord above.
You are always there when I need you
To lend a listening ear.

Whenever I thought I was going to fall
And that no one would be around to pick me up
Out of the shadows, you would come
Always there to break my fall.

Upon your lap, I used to sit
And listen to you talk.
I used to love to hear those tales
Of how you and mom fell in love.

And now that I'm a little older
But your baby just the same
I'd like to say I love you
And I'm grateful for you always.

That's My Mother

Independent and strong-willed
Beautiful, yet mild
Dedicated to being
One of a kind.
That's my mother.

Elegant and graceful
Always fighting to uphold
The beautiful children
She brought into this world.
That's my mother.

Peaceful and kind
A black rose
With her own mind.
Always willing to help someone shine.
That's my mother.

Loyal and true
Never showing when she's blue.
Binding our family together
Just like glue.
That's my mother.

To My Promise

If I can help by holding your hand, I will
But I can't yet 'cause I know that God has a master plan.
If I can help you see that you already have the victory, I would
But I know there are things that you need to figure out on your own.

If I can paint you a beautiful picture
I'll paint you a world where there's no pain
A world where you laugh while I dance
Where there isn't any care and no measure of fear.

If I could, I'll tell you that after God, you are my world.
I want to see your purpose fulfilled
I won't let you let go
If I could show you, I'll show you my heart.
I'll show you just how much I care because you are a very dear friend.

I'll show you that true love you deserve
Someone to stand with you
Someone who cares.

I hope to be a blessing
I hope that we can share
I hope that you'll choose me
And love me till the end.

Em City

Cold windy and flashing lights
Do you understand my plight?
Long days and longer nights
Cold, cold, cold
Why is it so cold?

Homeless people everywhere
How do they bear it?
How do they survive?
We weren't created to live like this
Someone, please tell me
How can they live like this?

They laugh and smile
But it is a fright.
They desire a home
But trade their money for heroin.
They trade their jobs for sex
Their norm is a paradigm I don't comprehend.

Their choices baffle me
Like why should I choose weed instead of being free?
What is addiction? Is it only to sex and drugs?
Do we only place stereotypes on things that differ from us?

By His Stripes

In the days of old, I remember a story being told
Of a beautiful baby born of a virgin mother
So far away in a manger
But the story doesn't end there, it gets quite unfair
As the earthly journey of our Saviour draws near.

He healed the sick
He raised the dead
And He caused the blind to see.
Gave love to the brokenhearted
Hope to the hopeless
And redeemed those lost in sin.

But despite it all
Some didn't think He was great
Because their hearts were filled with corruption and hate.
Crucify Him! They said
He's perverting our nation
And He claims to be the Son of God

So away they went with the old rugged cross
To the hill, they call Calvary.

He got one stripe for every time I'd tell a lie
One for every time I'd disobey.
One stripe for every time I got sick
One for every time I'd fall by the way.
One stripe for every time I wouldn't heed His voice
One for every time I'd sin
And make it seem like His coming was in vain.

However, the grave couldn't keep Him down

Chains and the stone couldn't have bound Him
His purpose was to die to the flesh and be risen in the Spirit.

As He ascended into Heaven
He promised us He'd return
And take us with Him to that place
Where streets are lined with silver and gold.

So we need to be patient and we need to be wise
Not living our life like those five foolish brides
But live our lives for Him and exalt His name on high.
Remembering that it was because of His love for us that He died.
But now He is risen and by His mercy and grace
We all have a chance to receive the gift of eternal life.

Dougla

Standing tall at five feet four
I walk around, my beauty is my pride.
Chest rise high, waist comes in
The fullness of my hips and thighs
Compliment my broad backside.
Born in a multicultural nation
Black, White, Indian, Portuguese and even Chinese.
My complexion the colour of a deliciously rich chocolate
Hair full and wavy
When stretched out touches my back.

Yet, the Indians whose blood flows through my veins
Tell me that I'm a disgrace
For my blood you see
Is mixed with that of the negroid race
To them, I'm a bastard child
And in their land, I have no rights.

My negro friends call me Indian
But their voice is filled with nothing but compassion.
They have accepted and loved me
And even though a bi-cultural person I may be
The motherland continues to open her hands out towards me.

My great grandfather was an indentured labourer
He came here on the last ship from India.
A beautiful negro was the one he favoured
And out of that love came my dougla grandfather.

Why should they shun someone who shares their blood?
Why can't they accept me for the person that dwells within?
A child of God
Born under two opposing cultures.
I was born so that we could be joined together.
Come! Let's step the discrimination against one another.

Behind these Prison Walls

I was confined to live behind these, prison walls.
Physical walls that were constructed to keep me, the enemy, away from society
In a place secluded with little access to friends and family
Because with little evidence and not enough money for good defense
I was deemed as someone who was not a law-abiding citizen.
The scum of the earth, as some would so liberally scream.
And to make matters worse my subconscious keeps telling me that this is all just a dream.

Behind these prison walls, I have had to grapple with hate.
Hate that runs so deep that it is nearly impossible to sleep
On the cold hard floors listening to fellow prisoners weep.
They weep for injustices, like being on remand for years
Not knowing when their matter would be heard.
But who am I, a self-proclaimed innocent, once, twice, or continuously repeat offender to complain about a failing justice system?

Behind these prison walls, I've lived a reality that many only see on T.V.
I can never fully express the magnitude of pain and trauma associated with

Living a life not only of physical but mental and emotional bondage.
I'm continually wrapped up and lost in thoughts of what-ifs and why me.
Longing for the day when I can go back and rewrite the script.
Maybe if I had chosen a different path, a different walk, or even to listen to a different song
Then maybe, possibly, I would not be at this place living in complete regret
Wondering if this is truly what was written on the cards for me.

Behind these prison walls in the stillness of time I mediate
My mind journeys back to simpler times.
I recall the innocence of childhood when living life seemed like such ease.
But amid that fantasy, a suppressed memory interjects
And I envision the days of limited resources and abuse that propelled me to run away from a home that failed to provide secure nurturing and covering.

The Wait

Those who wait on the Lord shall renew their strength.
That is what the Bible says.
But waiting isn't an easy thing
It's hard and takes determination to win.

I committed to waiting
But wow I did not see
That me waiting on you would turn out to be Him waiting on me.

In the wait, I am learning how to be still
I'm learning to seek and how to trust
I'm learning when to speak and gaining new insight
But most of all I'm learning that I don't always have to fight.

The wait is teaching me how to walk.
How to talk and how to shift my peripheral lens.
How to think outside the box and test those things that I thought were not.

If I can Change my Hair

If I can change my hair
I'd change nothing....
For my hair is simply an extension of my identity and who I was created to be.
Every curl and twirl remind me that while this journey may not be easy
I was born to live freely.

Yet, sometimes being born to live freely seems like a paradox.
When at times I'm mistreated for the crown that I wear.
It's as if my tresses ignite instant fear.
That's deep seated in ignorance
Mixed with a bit of unjustified arrogance.

See, for many years I lived by a set standard that said
Beauty was seen if my hair was straight and silky.
But how could that narrative be a reality
When it contradicts the uniquely diverse individual I was born to be?
For you see, my swaying hips and lustrous curls
Represent the merging of African and Indian heritages
That produced a one-of-a-kind Caribbean beauty.

If I can change my hair, I'd change nothing...
Cause to change my hair means that I have subtly chosen to reject me.
So, I'll say it again and I'll say it with flair;
If I can change my hair, I'd change nothing.

He Loves Me

I tried His patience
I left His place.
But His grace for me was never replaced
Because He loves me.

I went about from day to day
Never taking a moment to pray.
My mind, He would cross
Yet I failed to admit He is boss
But He still loves me.

Before I could fall, He'd grab my hand
An ever present help in my time of need.
But the outside world was desirable to me
So He decided to let me be.
Yet still, He loves me.

Now humbly I come
Begging Him to be
The merciful God that I know loves me.
His forgiveness I ask
And although coming back is a task.
It's a pleasure to say
I'm home! At last!

My Daddy, my Papa, my Oh…

He's my Daddy, my Papa, my oh….
The One who sustains me, who fashions me and clothes me.
The One who knew me before I knew myself .
He crowned me in royalty and calls me beauty.
When trials come and storms are rough
He sings to me a never-ending song of sweet serenity
That flows through the very residue of my soul.

My Daddy, my Papa, my oh…
My very best friend, the One upon whom I can truly depend.
He's my shield, my buckler, my strong defense.
I'm the apple of His eye, the one that He holds close.
When He rages war for me, none can contend.

He's my daddy, my papa, my oh…
An earthly representation of a heavenly King.
He provides for me and watches over me.
The foundation of the family
The one whose role was critical in shaping my identity.
The one who sat with me and told me numerous stories of old
His very blood runs through my veins.
And his expression of love for me motivates me to keep dancing in the midst of rain.

He's my daddy, my papa, my oh…
My daddy, my papa, my oh
My daddy, my papa, my oh
Without Him, I'd be truly lost.

Living a life wrapped up in bondage and deceived
Thinking that earthly brilliance can help me perceive
Spiritual treasures and mysteries.
But yet, He saved a wretch like me
And I'm eternally grateful that He redeemed me
My Daddy, my Papa, my oh…

Sound the Alarm

Sound the alarm.
The Lord's return is imminent.
Herald His voice, you who have been slothful.
Sound the alarm, the King is coming.
He is returning for a bride prepared for her groom.

He is coming.
Are you ready?
Don't let weariness consume you
After all the years you've tarried.
For the enemy is only out to deceive you.
Are you ready?
His beauty to behold.
He's coming to take you to a place where the streets are paved with gold.

But, we must be wise.
Don't be caught off guard, like the five foolish brides.
Though the trials seem countless
And the load you carry appears to be heavy
Even when the hearts of many wax cold.
"Look up!" He says, for your redemption draws nigh.

Redemption? How can it come from on high
When for years all I wanted to do was die.
Bound up in sin, wrapped in transgression, generational curses, too numerous to mention.
Have you ever been willing to fight?
But faced with constant battles of frustration, depression and oppression.

Sleepless nights, countless tears cried, searching for healing, but coming face to face with demons.

But then, the still small voice that says, My child Arise!
The sweet singing of Holy Spirit, over a broken and weary soul.
Being embraced by a Saviour, Jesus Christ my Redeemer
So now I dance and sing, I glorify His name
For I've been given beauty for ashes, strength for fear, gladness for mourning, peace for despair.

Today, this gift; the most precious gift of salvation, healing, deliverance and restoration is yours for the taking.
Do you hear Him knocking?
Can you sense the calling?
Open your heart, let Him in
For who the Son sets free,
Is free indeed!

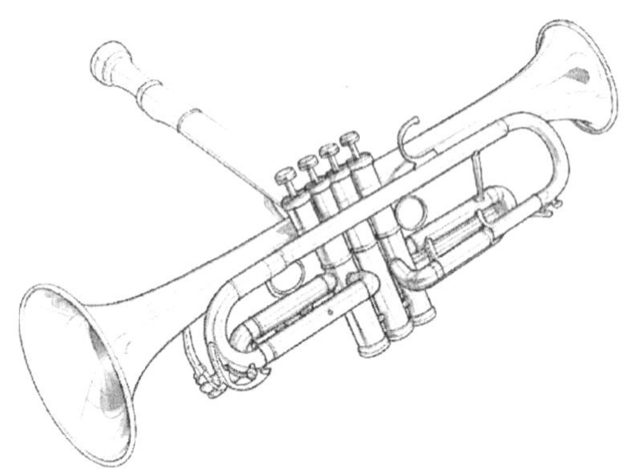

God's Got Me

For years I struggled with the fact that God loves me.
Simply because I hadn't truly experienced or maybe didn't fully understand love.
See, I'm a giver and I sometimes give sacrificially.
But, when it came to pouring back into me, it seemed that love was never really reciprocated.
Not to mention, the danger that came with me rejecting me.

Persons can say that they love you, but their actions and words don't always align.
Silly little me couldn't quite fathom the love God has for me.
So like the songwriter said, we look for love in all the wrong places
Aiming to fill insatiable voids
That can only be filled by our Creator, the lover of our souls.
Jesus the Christ, our righteous redeemer.

So if you're in a place where I once was
My encouragement is that you need a healer.
A healer who can, sing over the firmaments of your soul.
One whose beauty is foretold.
You my dear child, are in need of a friend.
A friend who will never leave you or forsake you.
One who will love you to the very end.

Let's not forget setting boundaries.
Saying no, is not a sin.
Release yourself from that bondage that tells you

That in order to be loved
You have to bend over backwards.
Your heavenly Father loves you
So much more than you can ever imagine.

Musings of a Worshipper

May my worship always come from a purified place that glorifies Your name.
A place of intimacy, where Your holy Spirit burns within me
And ignites a fire that causes the broken to be mended, the lame to walk, the blind to see and the deaf to hear.
Let the weight of Your power and glory flow through me.
Like a conduit that causes shackles to be broken and demons to flee.
May my song of praise forever glorify Your name.
The righteous One, the ancient of days.

The Fight

It's a fight for my sanity
But my God is right here with me.
He said in His Word, He'd never leave nor forsake
me.
When the road seems rough
And days and nights flow into one
The enemy tries to step in
With his chaos and constant pessing.
Rehashing dead scenarios
Like a broken record.
Crick crack, crick crack
Like he's trying to break my back.
Little does he know
That my praise is a mass weapon of war
So I fire hallelujahs
Knowing that he's already defeated.

Great strength lies within you
So, aim high and achieve your fullest
potential.
Believe in yourself and never loose
focus of your goals.

Xoxo Darcel

Made in United States
Orlando, FL
02 November 2024

53400225R00029